CONVOLUTED

Beth Parson

Library and Archives Canada Cataloguing in Publication

CIP data on file with the National Library and Archives

ISBN (trade paperback) 978-1-55483-581-2
ISBN (ebook) 978-1-55483-582-9

Dedicated to the magic of the universe.

CHAPTER
1
THE TOWER

Sensing the soil beneath me, I arrive at consciousness.

As I open my eyes, all I can remember is coming home from work, racing to get ready to go to the pub with Lyra and Van. My body heavily weighted on the ground underneath me tells me I never made it. The bed of mud feels uneven, wet and cold. Leaves and branches peel themselves from my bare legs as I roll to my side. Prying my heavy eyes open, I struggle to focus. The sun falling in the distance guides me as I pull myself to my feet.

Looking for anything recognizable, I head toward the light. A forest of trees surrounds me, more disoriented with every step. My fear boils to panic as I question how I got here.

Was I drugged? I must not have followed my mother's advice somehow. She always told me how to keep myself safe.

What have I done to end up here?

Stumbling with a lack of control of my body, my mind races at the thought of what dangers are out here, canting to catch me off guard.

The thought of my mother worrying in my absence sends memories of my childhood flashing in and out like a film in my mind. Knowing my mother would blame herself for the mess I am in now feels unbearable. I try to pry these thoughts from my head as they only add to my overwhelming sense of guilt stemming from some idiotic decision I must have made. Drawing attention to my feet, I retrace a meditation I once learned. I focused only on my physical body, sensing the existence of one limb at a time. My feet slip on every wet stone in the dirt, my mind in overdrive as I try to prevent a fall. Battling through my push-pull energy of fear and strength, I'm ready to let myself go, surrendering to the unknown. My heart races, knowing every morsel of my being comes down to my physical and mental strength. The will that derives from me is overtaken by fear swallowing me whole. Only I can save myself.

Flipping back to my deteriorating mental state, I repeat to myself, My name is Maggie. I chanted my introduction as if it were a mantra, helping me focus my mind as I moved through the terrain. Memories of my parents' separation interject the mantra like a flood in my mind without understanding the significance. I recall turning a corner in the hallway with the sound of their voices leading me to their presence at the front door. The abrupt silence when they noticed me said more words than any sentence they dare to whisper. Our front entrance was small. Small is the memory I created because that's how it felt standing between my mother and father. It was as if they were about to make a decision so serious that I could feel the fear radiating from them. It was nothing I felt before, being so young. On the verge of separation, the collective energy was finality, with no escape or control. Looking up at my father, I raised my arms, hoping he would pick me up and everything would be okay. In his arms, I scanned my mother's face for answers that led me to only one. He was leaving.

As I sat on the floor, tears streaming down my face, I remember asking myself if it was all my fault.

Knowing I can't stop moving to dwell on the cause of this, I direct my attention to my clothes to keep my mind in the present. White tank top, jean shorts, my worn-out shoes with no socks underneath, rubbing against my heels with every step. As the spirit of physical danger haunts me as I run, I fear my mind may be the true culprit in my demise. Unable to stop the memories, I am shown a vision of my mother and me in a new home shortly after the separation. Recalling an overheard phone conversation that I could not understand; only sensing nervous feelings. My mother's facial expression suggests concern for whoever is on the other end of the phone. Attentively listening, I hear the receiver returning to its base with a subtle click; she hung up. The look on her face could only be described as distraught. She pulls her hands to each side of her face, resting her fingertips on her temples, "Your father is coming to see us".

Stumbling more and more with each step forces my mind out of the memory reel and back to my physical reality. The sky is getting darker by the second. I am overwhelmed by the need to conjure up a plan that would help me evacuate this hell I'm trapped in. I am thirsty, with no water in sight. It's getting harder to run, and my feet are sore. My legs are so weak, but I know I have to push myself; I may never make it out of here. I have been running for an eternity, but I know only minutes have passed. The trees are closing in on me as my vision gives out. I am back on the ground once again, all hope lost.

I had no more fight left in me, as I felt a raindrop hit my cheek. I listen to the sounds of the rain hitting the ground while my soul is deprived of the will I need to get up. As the light rain turns into a sudden downpour, I am startled upward by the echo of raindrops landing with a splash. Rising to my feet, I move swiftly following the sounds of large rain droplets hammering onto water. Breaking through an opening in the trees reveals a stream in the distance. Sprinting to the shoreline, I follow the sounds of gushing water in hopes of reaching a waterfall. Dehydration drives my will, and I run faster, finally reaching flowing water. Gulping through the falls, I am unaffected by the torrential rainstorm that surrounds me.

Relieved, I know I must keep moving. Slipping and sliding, the wet terrain throws my footing out from under me, forcing me back to the ground. Placing my hands on my head, I close my eyes and lie still as I beg myself to try to get up. With my eyes thrown open to the sounds of someone thumping through the mud, a throbbing headache distracts me from the danger. As I take my hands off my head, I look down to see them covered in blood. Startled by the sounds of someone tearing through bushes like a bat out of hell, I pull myself to my knees and crawl forward, stabilizing myself. My impending danger drives the impulse to run. I am so scared to look back, but I know I must. I need to know how close they are. Tossing my head back and forth, I see nothing but darkness. Focused on the only senses still useful, my fear reaches its threshold at the sound of my name. One backward toss of my head, I glimpse a silhouette of a man not far behind.

Running as fast as I can, I wind in and out of trees to keep myself unseen. To no surprise, my foot gets caught in a branch, latching me to the ground as my body throttles forward.

With no anticipation, a sudden jolt strikes through my head, shocking me from head to toe. My ears begin to ring abruptly like an old dial-up modem. Unbearable pressure builds in my head, blurring my vision and distorting my mind. I brace myself in hopes that the worst is over, and like a flip of a switch, it stops. Losing consciousness, I lay in ruins.

CHAPTER
2
THE MOON

My eyes open, pierced by the blazing sun, feeling the warmth as it surrounds my body. My attention is focused on a healing sensation to my heels. As I place my hand on my head to feel for blood, I feel nothing at all. I take a deep breath in, filling my lungs. Exhaustion escapes my body.

Lying in this spot, I feel only relaxation. Fear has dissipated, and my anxiety is gone. I open my eyes to visualize the peace I feel. Reveling in my relief and peace, I think of the motion of a sway, like swinging on a porch swing. I must be on a boat. The light barrels in, piercing my eyes and obscuring the scenery around me. Placing my hand across my forehead to block the sun, I strain to gain focus as I sit up. My vision is becoming clear; I can see the ocean.

Realizing I am no longer in the forest, I am relieved to bask in tranquility. Confusing thoughts and memories of the forest interject my peace of mind. To sustain my sense of well-being, I assertively bring myself to my feet. Hypervigilant to everything around me, I ask myself who these people are and how did I end up on a boat?

The overwhelming struggle to understand takes hold of me, sending my body into a frantic state of quick movement. My feet move fast over a slippery deck, causing a predictable result. Limbs are thumping like being dragged over mounds of rock and dirt.

Suddenly, a man's voice calls out to me, followed by an aggressive yank upward by the back of my shirt. Startled by the sudden pull, I lay still. Minutes later, I can hear the voices of others surrounding me. The medical terminology identifies them as paramedics. The sound of a woman's ethereal voice guides my focus to her prominent features. Studying the face in front of me, my eyes are drawn toward her thin brown hair strands hanging free as if to escape from the hair tie; her hair falls perfectly down the sides of her face. Gently assisting me to my feet, she holds my shoulders to ensure my balance and whispers, "Trust in the Knight of Cups."

Unaware of the meaning of her words, I look to see if anyone is watching us in the distance. Distracted by other paramedics discussing my presence with the captain, I disregard her comment. Unable to find me as a cruiser on the ship, a room is offered to me anyway. Settling into my cabin, my refuted thoughts drive my curiosity.

Venturing out, I view a deck that wraps around the entire ship. Not far from where I stand, many people reside in first-class cabins all in a row. I attempt to lean over the railings to view the ocean.

A tap on my shoulder sends my head turning quickly to view the woman standing beside me, looking as though she was waiting for me to tell her something profound. She seems familiar, but I can't place her. An overwhelming feeling of familiarity washes over me as I scan her features. Abruptly, her red hair is thrown across her face as the entire boat comes to a crashing halt as if it hit something underwater. The woman is no longer in sight; am I hallucinating?

Passengers flee to the gates of the deck as the ship begins to flood. The cruisers burst into a frenzy, but the woman appears again in the distance. Looking at me as though she is waiting for my message, I peer into her eyes, realizing telepathy is no longer unimaginable. She softly speaking says, "I am here as I always am. You are protected."

As she turns away, I quickly scan the crowd around me. The boat sways out of control as chaos surrounds me. Rushing toward the woman's direction, the water gets deeper by the second.

Running becomes more difficult with each step as water gushes in. Crashing waves rise above my waist, almost completely immersing me underneath. I feel a scrape pierce through my wrist, catching it on the side of the boat. The water quickly rises over my lips, plummeting me underneath. Struggling to fight to the surface, another wave hurling through the ocean shoves me further underwater. Every longitudinal wave forces me closer to the seabed. My lungs fill with their last breaths as I am completely deprived of energy.

As my consciousness fades away and no will left to fight, feelings of guilt take over me. Believing I could have somehow changed this fate, I sink with shame. Unable to decipher if this reality is real, a parallel universe crosses my mind. I wish for this to all be a dream.

Slowly sinking further downward, I know I can't hold on any longer. Surprised by an aggressive yank upwards, I am suddenly pulled to the ocean's surface. Slammed on the boat deck, I lay still as I regained my breath. I gasped for air as the water inside me uncontrollably expels across the boat deck. My humanity returned with each breath, but I was dazed by the lack of a hero.

Disrupted by a sharp jolt to my head, ringing in my ears and pressure building leads me back down the path to unconsciousness.

What is happening?

CHAPTER
3
EIGHT OF SWORDS

Awakened to the sound of man's voice uttering, "Wake up!" followed by the slam of a door startles me upright. Little light in the room and no one in sight, I am distracted by a throbbing pain in my back and the cold, hard pavement beneath me. Now certain that the cruise ship was a dream, I stand slowly to view my surroundings. The sight of cement walls surrounding me sends panic rushing through my veins. The forest is my last true reality. I realize I must have been captured by the man chasing me. Continuing to observe my surroundings, I carefully run my hands across each cement wall in hopes of locating a door or window. The final wall leads my hand to fall shakingly upon a door handle. Quickly turning the handle in panic, only echoes bounce back as sounds of chains rattling from the outside. I am locked in!

Quickly going over each wall with my hands, I frantically searched for an escape. I stopped in my tracks by the sounds of fidgeting with the handle, the turn of a key and the click of a lock. Heart racing, I bolt to the corner of the room, crouching down. I try to make myself as small as possible. As I watch the handle turn, the door pushes open from the outside. A black work boot bulldozes through the door.

With a slam, a man comes through the door as if presenting himself to me as a hero. Walking swiftly toward me, I yell for him to stay away from me. With no regard to the imminent fear I exude, he reaches his hand toward me. Unable to release any words from my mouth, he stands over me as if devouring my thoughts.

Unable to decipher the features of his face, he speaks to me in a deep and distorted voice, "Do you know why you're here?" I struggle to respond as fear won't allow me to move or speak. He repeats himself numerous times without any response. The silence is broken when he says, "I was ordered to retrieve you."

Wondering what that means as he moves closer to me, I am quickly debilitated by another powerful jolt to my head, ringing in my ears and pressure building.

Through the suffering, I am unable to move as I feel his arms reach beneath me, pulling me up. One arm tense underneath my back, and he quickly snatched my legs, drawing upward underneath my knees. As the sounds of exiting a room fill my ears, I glance to the side, seeing darkness with a speck of light in a long corridor.
Unknowing of our destination, I may never find out.

Awakening to a room filled with images I could only assume are that of an old Paris hotel room, I see red and black pictures everywhere. I am laid across the largest bed I have ever seen, with a comforter full and thick stretched across. The comforter's corner has been pulled down, revealing black silk sheets underneath me. I glance to the walls covered with black and cream design and then to the ground, realizing red rose petals have filled the room.

I focus on my attire, cream-colored silk pants and a cream-colored shirt. I have no socks on my feet, but there's no mud or dirt in sight. Instincts send my arm around to check my head, with the surprising feel of a bandage. Quickly forcing my hand to the back of my heels, same thing - bandaged. I walk towards a mirror and carefully lift my silk pajama shirt to see if my back is clear. Bruises and scrapes reside all over but appear to be cleaned and cared for as my skin glows with hydration on top of the wounds. With my wrist bandaged, I have no idea how much time has passed or where I am. I wonder if the man who brought me here is protecting me. I sit at the edge of the bed with my head in my hands, trying to figure out what to do.

Rustling from outside the door interrupts my thoughts. I quietly peer through a tiny hole in the door, startled by a knock. I open the door to see a woman standing in front of me. I have seen her before.

CHAPTER
4
SUIT OF WANDS

With her features prominent, I recognize this woman. Memories of my dream on the cruise ship flash before me. I remember the two small strands of her hair falling freely down her face. She said something strange to me! How could this be if the cruise ship was a dream? She barges right past me into the room. I begin questioning her as she tries to explain that her presence is solely of a maid. She rushes back to the door to pull in a cart of the most perfectly presented food I have ever seen. Adamant for answers to my questions, I press on. She interrupts every question I put forward, each time demanding me to eat. Frustrated with her purposeful answers lacking clarity, my eyes quickly shift to the open door, running as fast as I can toward it. Examining everything ahead of me, I make it to a hallway resembling the same theme in my room. Frantically hammering on every door as I yell for help, no one responds. A bright exit sign fills my vision as I reach the end of the hallway.

Charging into the exit door, misery grabs a hold of me as the door I try to shove open brings me to a halt; locked. I turn around, bolting down the hallway, beating each door. Almost back to where I started, the woman stands calmly watching from outside the room. Nowhere else to go, I am deadlocked in fear. Her stare forces me to focus inward, wishing I was invisible as my eyes close tightly. Hoping for wish fulfilment of another reality, my emotions build from despair to strength. Captivity is seemingly the only consequence, I open my eyes, ready to fight for another outcome. Scanning the corridor again, I see hope in a flicker of light behind her. Knowing it may lead to a possible escape, I have to try. Pulling a painting from the wall, I charge forward. Running toward her as fast as I can, the painting held high, ready to swing, she walks slowly toward me. Focusing on the light and then back to her, I am shocked to no longer see her in my view, as if she disappeared into thin air. Confused, I continued to run toward the light. Turning the corner, a door before me sends me bursting with a sense of freedom.

Defeated, the other side of the door reveals the woman standing before me. She says, "There is no escape." Frightened by her impossible supernatural disappearing act, I am scared to know what she will do to me now. Grabbing my arm firmly, she pulls me back toward the room. Wary of each step, whilst surrendering to my doom, she tells me the freedom I seek is not allowed.

Tears roll down my face as I sit on the bed. I plead, please tell me why I'm here. Holding my shoulders, she says, "The answers will come to you. Be patient. I have clear instructions that I have to follow. Get some rest." Walking toward the door, she glances back and whispers, "You're not the only one." With no chance to respond, she shuts the door, locking it from the outside.

Recollecting everything I experienced, I think of the forest, my parents, and the ship. Self-deprecating thoughts still convince me this is somehow all my fault. Mental exhaustion leads me to bed. Finally shutting my eyes, I realize I didn't turn out the light. I repeatedly tell myself to get up and turn it off, too tired to move. Annoyed by the brightness in the background of my tightly closed eyes, my frustration reaches its boiling point. Just as I slam my eyes open, the light suddenly turns off.

Vicariously understood, I know I am being spied on through a type of surveillance preposterous to anyone.

CHAPTER
5
TEN OF CUPS

I am awakened by the sound of keys rattling in the lock. I jump out of bed, focus on my presentability, and quickly snap myself back to the reality of a potential threat to my safety. I am petrified as a man walks through the door, quickly shutting it behind him. Frozen in time, he steps carefully toward me, shocked by his remarkable calming energy, and abruptly relieves me of imminent danger.

His gentle smile propelled toward me, and my eyes quickly scanned every semblance. His crystal blue eyes met mine, I was astounded at the sudden strike of an extraordinary sense of connection bringing us together. To say it was love at first sight wouldn't be enough to describe the vibration between us.

Finding it increasingly difficult to hold my composure, he introduced himself as Zane. With no response from me, he proceeded to speak. "Your stay here will be long enough to ensure you understand your destiny." His energy exudes chemistry with mine, but his word choice feels instructed. With no comparable experience in life, I stand quietly in awe, waiting for him to say more.

Appearing unaffected by our connection, he pulls a black pager from his pocket and navigates through clicks to show me what to press in an emergency. He pauses suddenly to ask, "Do you understand?"

His lack of reaction has me questioning my thoughts and intuition, triggering a lack of trust. Fight or flight takes over me as I feel the urge to dart past him toward the door, which sends me flying directly toward him. He quickly grasps hold of me, locking his arms around mine as if I am confined in a straight jacket. His lips rested outside my ear. I know I must succumb to his strength as he quietly whispers, "Listen to me, or you will die. I understand what you are feeling."

His voice leaves me placid as he slowly eases his grip around me. In his arms, trust is restored, and my intuitiveness tells me he is also astonished by his inexplicable presentiment toward me, leaving us both inarticulate. As I sit voiceless, he stands slowly as he moves backward toward the door. Tenaciously masking the epiphany, he whispers, "Please be patient, you will understand everything soon, if you need me I will find you." My eyes scan his every move as he sets the pager on the side table before walking out the door. Ambiguous feelings fill my soul, ascending me to a space lost in reverie.

Laying on the bed, with the ceiling as my focus, I am startled by a knock on the door. I laboriously walk to the door, opening it to see a much-anticipated familiar face. The unnamed woman stands there with noticeable self-condemnation. I feel annoyed by her previous lack of effort to clarify, standing firm before letting her in. Sensing my unapproachability, she delicately introduces herself to me as Carina.

Intrigued by what else she may reveal, I alter my demeanor and sway my arm, inviting her to enter. She speaks quickly as she enters, explaining she is aware of my encounter with Zane. I stand patiently, listening as she explains her presence to me. "I only have a minute. I will respond when you need me. Please use the pager."

With sincere affinity, I nod in affirmation.

As Carina turns to exist, I ask her why she will not speak to me. With no response, I asked her why she would let me know she was aware of my interaction with Zane without providing relevance. My thoughts tell me her statement was meant to trigger a reaction. Wondering why she would want me to know she was aware leads me to conclude it as a warning or that Carina and Zane may not be on the same journey.

Carina responds, "My statement was meant to tell you that nothing here is a secret. I have been watching over Zane his whole life. Everything that happens, I know. I must go now."

Rushing toward the entrance, the sound of the lock clicking in my ears leaves me no chance to dig deeper.

Hours slowly creep by, leaving me restless and bored. Gazing through the window, the beautiful endless sky is my solace. With little food around, I wonder when my next meal will arrive. Carefully reaching for the pager, I want to test it out.

As I begin to type, a sudden craving is triggered by a memory of when I would meet Lyra and Van at the pub. We ordered the same meal as if it were tradition. Meeting at the same time each week gave us all something to look forward to, while we navigated our worlds.

Reviewing the food list before clicking send, Carina's ethereal voice calls out to me from outside the door. "Maggie, I have your dinner." Rushing to meet her in the entranceway, I immediately noticed that the precise selection of food matches my memory of our traditional weekly meal. Knowing I did not send the message, I am perplexed.

Carina moves quickly to exit the room. Astounded, I stare at the food before me, asking myself how this could be possible. Remembering her unexplained disappearance in the hallway leaves me certain she is reading my mind.

CHAPTER
6
TWO OF CUPS

Another morning awakening to a surreal presence. Thoughts of how my mother would be feeling without me, sickened me.

I paged Carina as I was accustomed to, except Zane entered the room. Standing firmly, he holds a garment bag folded neatly over his arm. Fulfilling my need to quickly alleviate him from holding the gift so flawlessly draped, I take the bag from his clasp.

Fidgeting with his cufflinks, I notice his eyes shift toward his wrist. Removing his watch, he places it in my hand. I can hear his heart beating through his chest as he assembles his thoughts to ask, "Will you join me for dinner tonight at 6 pm?" Holding the watch in my hand, I am gratified to see it's precisely 11:11. Remembering thought-provoking conversations with Lyra and Van, they were always intrigued by the relevance of recurring numbers signifying angel numbers as guidance from the divine.

Unable to ignore the message, I accepted Zane's offer with trust.

He smiles with a wink that leaves me fantasizing; I am so drawn to his charm.

Left alone to perceive the meaning of all of this, I stare at the hands of the clock, trying to recall the last moment I was aware of time.

Eagerly anticipating what will come of our next union, I rush to the shower to prepare. After all the beautifying was finished, I reached for the garment bag. Intuitively expected, the dress appeared perfect before me; most beautiful in color, shining like the stars, the perfect fit. Critiquing myself in every mirror, I notice that my wounds have healed miraculously. I pull my hand to my head, realizing the injury sustained in the forest is gone. Shifting my focus to my wrist, the scrape has disappeared. With no trace of injuries, I wonder how this could be possible.

I glance at the watch, it's now 6 pm. I hear sounds at the door, right on time.

Zane enters the room with a marvellous expression. I can sense his allure toward me. Modestly smiling, I thanked him for the gift. Observing his strikingly perfect eyebrows, my eyes fall downward, meeting his as they pierce through my soul to the hilt.

Frenzied by the intensity between us, I quickly shifted my eyes from him to the floor.

I lift my head to his enamoured voice, asking, "Would you like to go now?" I responded with a quiet yes and walked towards him. He put his left elbow forward in an effort to have me link my arm with his. Searching my soul as we walked in union through the doorway, I wondered what it was about him that made me forget everything. The chemistry between us was beyond everything I had experienced in this life.

He led me to the end of the hall where the exit sign shines. The door was previously locked when I tried to escape. Reaching into his pocket, he pulled out a key and motioned for me to move ahead. I walked carefully through the door, unaware of what I would enter into. He followed closely, giving me a sense of safety.

We proceed carefully up the stairs with him holding my arm tightly. We reached the top. Zane held the door open, revealing the most perfect rooftop.

CHAPTER
7
TEMPERANCE

Amid a few round tables beautifully decorated, I focused on the black drapery falling perfectly over them. Gazing toward the centerpieces, displayed a single red rose in each vase.

Zane took my hand and led me to our table directly in the middle of the rooftop. With his cavalier demeanor, he pulled out my chair as I sat. His eyes locked in mine, as he returned to his seat, asking if I was comfortable. Affirmatively nodding while viewing the rooftop, I notice a door wide open, leading to a stairwell. Glancing back and forth between Zane and the stairwell, an older man strangely appears in the doorway. Dressed in a suit, balancing a round tray carrying drinks, he approaches our table, gently placing our wine in front of us. Without speaking, he calmly turns away toward the stairwell. His lack of communication made it feel as though his presence was watchful versus catering. Zane, non-reactive to the peculiarness, pours the wine.

When he lifted his glass to take his first sip, I followed his lead. As we placed our glasses back on the table, Zane adjusted the cufflinks on his suit as though something was irritating him. Remembering him doing this the first time he entered my room, I asked him why his attention was drawn to his cufflinks.

Suddenly, a familiar ringing in my head again. I try to conceal any obvious reaction to the pain. As I anticipated its momentum, the sensation quickly halted, leaving me with a feeling of control.

Zane, unaware of my episode, looked up at me from his cufflinks. After a pause, he said, "I was trying to be discreet, while on a trip with Carina, I somehow pierced my wrist." He shifted his body towards me, deflecting further questions from me, he said, "You must have so many questions. I would like you to keep them for now. Instead, will you tell me what you remember?"

Memories of the dirt path suddenly flashed before my eyes. Ready to tell him everything, I restrained myself as the waiter re-approached our table. Zane barely acknowledged his food as I proceeded to particularize my experience. He listened carefully, observing me closely as I spoke.

After my lengthy elucidation, Zane stood up from the table as he reached to pull my chair toward him. With endearment, he brushed his hand softly down my arm until he reached my hand. Gently pulling me up from my chair, he stood confidently in front of me. Our eyes locked as he slowly leaned toward me and whispered, "I am sorry for what you are going through, but it will all become clear in time. I need to take you back to your room."

Walking back to the room, I feared being alone again. Unable to control my emotions, tears rolled down my face. Standing at the doorway, our mutual gaze was broken as he turned to leave. As my heart sank, he quickly turned back to wipe the tears from my eyes and said, "I promise you we are very similar. I need time to find answers."

CHAPTER
8
THE HANGED MAN

I threw myself backward on the bed, landing in a surprisingly comfortable spot. Taking a deep breath in, I release it with a forceful sigh. I closed my eyes tightly, searching my soul for gratitude while dodging ruminating thoughts. Cycling through Zane's words that alluded to our similarity left me baffled. To clear my mind, I guided myself into meditation. As I ascend, it feels as if my body is slowly rising from the bed, settling into a float. Muffled voices and sounds of laughter enter my mind, disengaging me from tranquility.

I transitioned out of meditation, slowly moved my fingers across the comforter beneath me, but I am stalled by the feeling of the woolsack was no longer full and thick. Apprehensive, I sat up to view my surroundings. Where am I now? Did I drink too much wine and not notice we entered a different room?

Once again in unfamiliar territory, I look around at the multitude of doors and windows. Fighting panic, I tell myself these exits provide me with a chance to escape. Failing at every attempt, I stand desperate at the final door.

Thoughts of Zane flow through my mind. I wondered if he knew I was there. The final door clicks open. I'm frozen, staring at the open space between the door and its frame. I slowly pushed the door open, revealing Zane in front of me.

My initial euphoria dwindles as he walks past me through the door, radiating a cold and intimidating energy. I can't help but wonder what or who is triggering his negative vibration. Choosing my steps carefully to stay out of his energy field leaves me backed into a corner. What seems like an effort to pull me out, he wraps his hand around my wrist. Startled by the identical sensation to what I felt on the cruise ship, I quickly pulled my arm from Zane's grasp, startling him with an epiphany. Suddenly, the memory of Zane telling me he pierced his wrist on a trip with Carina hits me with an epiphany of my own. Our dual reaction to the same astonishing revelation has me wondering about Zane's intentions. I ask myself how our experiences could be parallel when my captivity screams that our power is not balanced. Unable to understand his intentions, sent me fleeing to make a break for it and running straight to the door. Zane yells, "Maggie, stop!" just as Carina appears, blocking the doorway. Zane's face washed out, he moved quickly past me and around Carina, leaving us facing the door.

Carnia, held a garment bag, forcefully pushed forward into the room. I was jostled backward, leaving her time to quickly shut the door behind her. I restored my balance as she lay the bag on the bed. Turning back toward me, she demanded I get ready and stormed out of the room. Staring at the shut door in front me, I noticed a tarot card pushed through the bottom of the door. Bending over to view an upright Knight of Cups, I reached to pick it up. Just about to grab the card, an invisible force pulled the card back through the crack in the bottom of the door. Startled by the supernatural force and unable to decipher the message, I knew that Carina was not who she said she was.

Again, the sense of some preposterous surveillance washed over me.

Surrendering to this fate, I pulled a beautiful red dress from the bag. Changing quickly, I stood in front of the mirror and critiqued myself. Miraculously, my skin was radiated like never before. I looked so full of life. I told myself I was ready to go.

Within seconds, Zane walked through the door.

Appearing calm and collected, he said, "I heard you were ready." He extended his left elbow for me to link my arm in his. Relieved his energy was once again welcoming, I wrapped my arm around his as we exited the room.

The celestial connection between us felt exactly as it was earlier on the rooftop. Overwhelmed by the extraordinary protective energy he exuded, I willingly followed his lead. He walked me through a tunnel to an open car door. I turned my head quickly making eye contact. Falling into a moment's gaze, I had all the affirmation I needed to get in the car.

The car ride was silent, which led me to think to myself. I remembered Zane's words, "I heard you were ready." Puzzled by the context, I sifted through every memory leading up to his arrival. Knowing I was alone in my room, I asked myself, how did he hear?

As the car slowed to a stop, I was amazed by the sight of a castle before me. Feeling Zane observing me, I quickly turned to face him. In wonder of his supernal spirit, my eyes met his, locked in an unexplainable gaze. As the driver brought the car to a stop, Zane raised his hand to receive mine. He said, "Maggie, it's time."

Walking toward the castle, with my arm linked underneath Zane's, was an exact depiction of a fairytale. The doors magically opened as we approached, leaving me in awe. Upon entering, exhilaration ran through me as I looked up to a ballroom filled with people.

CHAPTER
9

VIII
STRENGTH

As I assimilated everyone in the room, I was awestruck by the elegance surrounding me. My attention shifted toward those portraying an indescribable beauty and nonentity in my world. Admiral attire left me mystified as each delicate gown perfectly hit the floor. Every suit I saw was debonair, truly a spectacle.

Holding on tightly to Zane as he guides me toward the bar, I am distracted by the ricochet of glances thrown our way.

Equally captivated by those surrounding me, I am fixated on a woman smoking an opera-length cigarette. Curious to know her story, questions spiralled through my mind. With every new question in my mind, more glances seem to come my way as if my thoughts provoked attention.

Zane reached through the crowd to pass me a drink, saying, "You are going to need this." With a quick smile, he turned back to the man behind the bar. Conversing with him, I continued to look around at the scenery before me.

Sipping my drink, my eyes scan the faces surrounding me. Every face I meet sends a sudden rush of different energies radiating toward me and transforming into voices in my mind. Feelings of empathy exude from some glances as they mutate to warning voices. Sounds of laughter heckling through my thoughts come from an eerie negative energy dispelling from others. Feeling overwhelmed by this unfamiliar experience, I wonder if I am losing my mind.

I am quickly propelled back by the sudden sense of Zane's watchfulness. He leads me to a staircase as if to end my fixation on the crowd. We stood together, gazing at what looked like a thousand steps winding to a peak. Peculiarly, a woman stood as a statuette on every other step.

The intimidating scene is contrast indicative of their angelic beauty. Their exquisite, radiated skin left me disarranged. Deep in my thoughts, I was startled as Zane slowly unlocked his arm from mine. He retrieved my drink from my hand and placed it on a table beside us. Taking two steps backward, he left me at the bottom of the stairs. Words unneeded to be said, I knew I was meant to climb the staircase alone.

Taking my first steps carefully, I feel apprehensive about moving to join the first woman. She stares sharply into my eyes, leaving me conscience-stricken as I proceed up the stairs. Perspicaciously, I climb each step, observing subtle energies as I go.

Sudden jolt struck in my head as I quickly turned to view the bottom of the staircase. Insecure by the thought of continuing the climb, I looked for reassurance in Zane's eyes.

Just as the ringing in pressure built, his deep gaze was hypnotizing, quickly advanced to thought transference. "Maggie, I feel it too. You need to run." Zane saying he feels it too resonates as a surprising confession. With no time to process, his telepathic instruction sends me running up the remainder of the staircase. Mystified by my seemingly growing ability to communicate telepathically, my heart races in panic. Stalled by the sound of a commotion, I turn back to check on Zane. Men have surrounded Zane; he disappears from my sight. As I was about to take a step back toward him, the woman sharing my step barricaded herself in front of me. Her voice sternly in mind said, "Try it." Threatened by her aggressiveness, I compliantly turned to continue up the stairs. Reaching the top, I was met by the last woman. Positioning herself beside me, she walks me toward a door as if she was delivering me to someone.

Pushing it open, she shoved me through the doorway, leaving me stumbling to catch my footing. I looked up immediately to see in front me the odd man who served us our dinner that night on the rooftop.

Sizing him up, he disturbingly said, "Maggie, I have been waiting for you."

CHAPTER
10
SEVEN OF SWORDS

Sensing the ringing and pressure dissipating, I try to grasp hearing my name come from a man I don't know. Desperate for answers, my despondent expression prompts him to introduce himself. "My name is Conway Clarke." Discontented, I quickly dictate the dialogue, asking him why I am here. Just about to move right into another question, he sternly interrupts me, offering me a seat. Refusing the seat, he calmly walked to his parlor. Reaching for a bottle of whisky, he sets two glasses on the counter. With Conway occupied by mixing a drink, I walked around the room while studying every inch. Admiring the leather furniture perfectly situated around a crystal table, I am fascinated to see water bubbles flowing back and forth between the glass top.

The crackling sound of whiskey pouring over ice directed my attention back to him. Walking toward me with drinks in hand, I was astonished by his appearance. His grey hair indicated he was much older than me. However, his skin appeared unaged.

Demanding I take a seat, I settled into the couch across from him. I sat quietly, intimidated by the thought of initiating any further conversation while he placed the drinks on the table between us.

I watched as he took a sip of his whiskey, then firmly placed it back on the table. Breaking the silence, he said, "You must have so many questions?" I nodded my head in response. He continued to speak. "Your turn will come, give me the opportunity to explain. You may ask questions when I have finished speaking. Understand?" Attentively listening, I nodded in confirmation.

"The night you were running down the dirt path, I know you remember your foot getting caught in the branch sending you to the ground. What you don't remember is smashing your head on a rock that completely knocked you unconscious as your body rolled downhill through mounds of dirt and rock, landing you in the river. The man chasing you tried to catch you by grabbing your shirt. Unable to pull you against the current, the water drew you from his grip. Forced to the edge of a waterfall, logs and debris were crashing into you as you sank. With one more aggressive yank of your shirt, he was able to bring you to the surface, pulling you to safety."

My mind flashes back to the night on the rooftop with Zane, leaving me skeptical. I know this man may have been eavesdropping as I shared my experience.

Going with the flow of his interpretation, I recalled my time on the dirt path. Understanding I was missing the details of how I got from the dirt path to the cell I woke up in, his story filled in the blanks. Memories of my physical experiences on the cruise ship seemed comparable to his description of what happened to me. When I fell on the boat deck, I remembered feeling as though I was being dragged over mounds of dirt and rock. My memories of drowning were comparable to his description of what happened to me in the river. While I piece together all the details, the vision of the woman appeared to me in a vivid flash. Panic washed over me, throwing me to my feet as I suddenly remembered her face; the same face as the woman who walked me to the door of this room! Conway stood abruptly, staring directly in my eyes he said, "You remember the woman."

As I sat back down, an overwhelming sense of intrusion came over me.

Conway walked towards me, and looked directly into my eyes as if he were looking through me. As he approached, I carefully moved sideways off my seat, standing once again as I slowly moved away from him. Knowing I had nowhere to go, I shut my eyes tightly, wishing he would disappear before I opened them. Holding them shut, I listened to his breath. My heart beat heavily as he whispered in my ear, "Maggie, stop thinking, I will not hurt you."

I opened my eyes slowly to see Conway's non-reactive expression, I was consumed with fear. He turned toward the door, breaking the intense fear binding me to my thoughts. Opening the door, he called out, "Please come in."

Stunned, I looked at the woman I was rushing toward on the ship. Guiding her leisurely toward me, he said, "This is not how I planned to deliver what I want you to know. However, I can see your need for answers regarding this woman is causing you distress."

"Maggie, meet Vina."

CHAPTER
11
THE REVERSED MAGICIAN

Reaching her hand toward mine in introduction, I couldn't help but notice her red hair falling perfectly, brushing across her collarbone as she went. A glimmer of what felt like deja vu took hold of me; a past life experience. I knew her.

I felt calm in her presence. She had a smile that lit up the room. Shaking her hand left me feeling starstruck without entertainment. Taking a seat beside me, with my hand in hers, she softly said, "Please listen to everything I say, so I can help Conway compose the right words to explain to you why you are here."

Delicately removing her hand from mine, she stood slowly. Walking to the parlor, she glided her fingers over every bottle as if to feel a vibration from the one she should choose. Slowly grasping the neck of a dusty bottle of wine, she effortlessly pulled the cork out.

Keeping her eyes focused on the wine as she poured, followed by a swirl and then a slow sniff. Appearing blissful, she took a sip. Pleased, she looked at me and said, "Let's go have dinner."

Opening the door, she waved for me to follow as she disappeared. Quickly following her lead, I entered a room to a perfectly set dinner table. Conway followed close behind saying, "Please sit. Dinner will arrive shortly."

Seated, copious amounts of food were placed in front of us, covering every inch on the table. Serving completed, each server stood in silence as if waiting for permission to leave. Focused only on Conway, he shifted his eyes toward the left. Following his subtle command, they quickly vanished from the room. Conway looked up at Vina. He nodded as if to give approval for her to start speaking.

Vina looked at me while she sipped her wine. She placed her glass on the table and said, "Hush your mind, you need to listen. I was a friend of your father's."

Triggered, I yelled across the table at her. What do you mean? Where is my father and what have you done to him? In an effort to control the situation, Conway slammed his fist down on the table, forcing the plates to rebound as every glass rattled across the table. He sternly said, "Silence, you will not interrupt again, or you will regret it." I was frozen with fear again, Vina spoke softly, "You will remember me by the time this dinner is over."

Conway's belligerent behavior evoked a memory of a story once told to me by my father. I recall hearing an argument between my mother and father, provoking me to question my father. Being very young, I still knew he worried about how his articulation would affect me. Carefully choosing his words, he talked about a man my mother disapproved of. He explained, he thought he could trust him, but my mother disagreed. He said their relationship caused friction between him and my mother. Trusting his instinct, he stated that his relationship with him was not blind to my mother's concerns. However, he needed to continue for the greater good. Sending me on my way to play, I remember thinking I did not like the man that caused this arguing between my parents.

Avoiding eye contact with Conway, I picked at the food before me. Vina suddenly said, "I have certain gifts your father helped me understand. I am not only a mind reader, but I have abilities that allow my soul to travel outside my body and enter anyone's dream state appearing in my physical form. I have been watching you since your birth. This is why you remember me. Appearing to you in your dreams and reading your thoughts was my job. Something different happened recently."

Feeling violated after hearing that my every thought was monitored since birth, I quickly looked away. Remembering Carina telling me she had watched over Zane his whole life left me with an uncanny feeling of similarities between us. With Conway uncomfortably staring at me, I looked back at Vina.

Vina continued, "We ordered a man to bring you here. I know you remember everything that happened on that dirt path the night you were brought here. When you hit your head, you passed out, sending you into a dream state. The interesting thing is that I did not come to you in that dream you pulled me into it. I don't understand how you compelled me into your dream. I am confused. We have so much to learn from each other." Pausing to take another sip of wine, she placed the glass back on the table. "Please speak now, Maggie."

CHAPTER
12
THE FOOL

I was triggered by Vina telling me she had been listening to my thoughts since I was born, sending me on a trip through memory lane. Drowning in my thoughts, I remembered when I was young in the car with my parents. Singing along to a song on the radio, they seemed happy. Not knowing all the words but giving it my best shot, I sang along with them. Stumbling through the lyrics, I swore along with the artist. I am sure my parents heard as they laughed through to the next chorus. Raised not to swear, the innocent singing of lyrics sent me spiraling through a mess of guilt. Swallowed by anxiety, I remembered having a hard time overcoming the shame I felt.

Finding myself in that same thought process as I grew older taught me how to adapt to those thoughts on my own. Learning that someone was listening to every thought I ever had filled my soul with dread. Permitting themselves to paint their own picture, transgression infringes my rights as a human being.

Once again, I was startled by a jolt to my head, followed by a voice in the distance. Difficult to focus, I placed my hands over my ears.

Conway, standing nearby, yelled, "Stop thinking!"

Discomfort fading away, I removed my hands from my head. Immediately moving my hand to my wrist, dismayed by a familiar tingling sensation. Remembrance of Zane describing a similar sensation impelled my inquiring mind. Instantaneously, Zane's dulcet voice transfused my mind. "You have to get out of there."

Flashing before my eyes, penetratingly discerning, I am shown a vision of an upright Knight of Cups. The same card appeared in the hotel after Carina slammed the door.

Looking up at Conway, I masked my expressions, I hoped he could not sense or hear my connection with Zane. Backing away, he moved across the room. Unemotionally, he turned his head toward me and said, "It's now time I tell you." Sharpening my sereneness, I desperately responded in approval.

"I know you remember the day that your dad left you and your family."

"Do you remember looking out the window after your father left your home?"

Flashing back to that day, I remembered running to the window and pulling back our heavy accordion-like curtains as he left. Quick visions flash in my mind as I recalled him being led by a man wearing a suit. He placed his hand over my father's head, he guided him into the car without option. Overwhelmed by the vision reel, I felt a sense of relief as the pieces come together. Explaining the day to Conway felt intrusive. Conway interjects my thoughts with another question, "When was the last time you heard from your father?"

Disclosing the details of the last phone call I remembered between him and my mother left me feeling disloyal. Conway appeared shocked after learning that my father said he was coming to see us. Without inquiring, I quickly added that he never showed up.

Puzzled, he fidgeted as he leaned back into his seat and then forward, placing his elbows on his knees. Uttering suddenly, "Your father is partly responsible for everything happening here."

CHAPTER
13
HIGHER POWER

I waited to hear Zane's voice on the forefront, as I shifted my focus back to Conway. Placing his whisky back on the table, he raised his head to speak. "Let me explain. Your father and I studied Biochemistry, genetics and molecular biology together. Our studies led us to research projects all around the world and we met many scientists along the way, gaining knowledge with every interaction. On the advice of one revolutionized scientist, we arrived at an underground center of artifacts. We stumbled across a blueprint of an ancient experiment that claimed humans could develop a higher state of being. We vowed to keep this discovery hidden, knowing this blueprint was never meant to be found. With good intentions, we tossed ideas around for months, brainstorming ways to convince the world to grant us the permission to follow the experiment in the artifact.

"Knowing scrutiny would be present in our strictly science results world, we started working on a proposal, anyway. The proposition to the board of the university, if approved, would ultimately allow us permission to carry out testing on willing humans in accordance with the directions of the artifact. After numerous discussions, we decided never to submit it, in fear of rejection and the artifacts confiscation afterward. With curiosity fueling our drive, we chose another route. We trusted our most loyal friends to help us decipher our findings.

"To our disappointment, we noticed a page missing. After careful consideration, we decided we had enough evidence to move forward with the experiment. We thought if our experiment was successful, we could offer humans an extraordinary life experience.

"Our small loyal group became a full-blown secret society. Welcome to our fortress."

Conway paused and moved across the room. Appearing deep in thought, he poured another drink. Questions swirling through my mind, I remained silent in fear any interruption would sidetrack the flow of information.

I found myself in a hypnotic state, a rush of what felt like divine magic filled me. Pins and needles light up my skin, and a sense of Zane's presence washes over me. Butterflies flowed through my stomach, expecting to see him enter the room. Nowhere in sight, I wondered if we are experiencing the same phenomenon simultaneously.

Disguised, I focused directly on Conway returning to his seat. Motioning for Vina in the distance to join us again, she approached slowly. Sitting beside me, her eyes locked on Conway as if awaiting her next instruction.

Breaking his eye contact with Vina, he spoke directly to me.

"The artifacts proved that we could create a higher state of being by obtaining DNA from the most extraordinary. Simply put, it ultimately creates an injectable serum igniting every recipient's most sought-after intelligence, talents and supernatural gifts.

"We investigated the most incredible people, creating a list of candidates. Choosing to invite only those with proven capabilities brought us Vina. Known for her clairvoyance, telepathy, and precise accuracy through tarot and astrology, we had to reach out. Vina was an impeccable candidate, agreeing to our terms of the testing. She agreed to keep our investigation secret and be willing to cut herself off from the outside world. So we continued down the list, extending our invitations with Vina by our side. Each candidate accepted, with high hopes of us creating something viable to heighten the human state being.

"Following the blueprint, we understood we created two serums with two separate groups of individuals. Each group of recipients excelled in the same fields.

"Our serum was created from candidates leading the healthiest lifestyles. Discovering many exceptional stories, we chose those with the most amazing health phenomena. One person had never experienced the symptoms of a common cold. Another, alive and well at the age of one hundred and twenty.

"Retrieving DNA from candidates proving the highest forms of intelligence was next. Your father and I travelled to many countries, identifying intelligence in many forms. Political, religious, spiritual, practical and academic.

"The DNA donated for youth longevity was obtained from mature people showing no signs of aging, exceptional facial symmetry and undeniable radiant skin.

"Your father chose the candidates for the first serum. I chose the candidates for the second serum. Each serum contained DNA from the most supernatural, intelligent, healthy and youthful humans on earth.

"Eager to test our findings, we injected ourselves with our serum.

"Our results produced different outcomes. I seemed to resist a common cold, developing supernatural abilities such as telepathy, and appeared to look younger, however, my contrasting grey hair showed error.

"Your father seemed to develop an extreme academic excellence, able to decipher scientific findings easily. However, he suffered from depression greatly.

"We realized the system was not perfect."

Silence filled the room with an eager anticipation for a response from me. Counteraction waiting to fill the void of silence appeared ethereal in my lack of response. I felt charmed that they may have created something magical, I am enlightened by the discovery of something supernatural. Knowing that logic and fear were expected of me, I sat in gratitude for hope that their inquest provided proof of some form of magic on earth.

Conway ignored my silence and continued, "Infatuated with our personal progress, we wanted to give others the opportunity to test the serum. Choosing from one of the two created, we injected those willing.

"We quickly realized we fell short in our testing. Recipients started to report negative psychological effects. Completing a grueling assessment of each individual, we were reminded of an irreversible truth. Good cannot exist without evil. The serum comprised of many cells with magnificent anomalous abilities, also accompanied cells with adverse emotional distress. Assessments confirming mania, delusions, and paranoia were on the rise seemingly bringing along more negative side effects.

"With no certain cure, we kept researching, hoping for a miraculous result."

Vina interjected, "As you know, I am one of two candidates who was invited here with supernatural abilities, the other person is my sister, Carina."

Recalling my time spent with Zane and Carina, I was relieved by my accurate intuition that Carina was not who she said she was. Learning Carina was part of all this, triggered my memory of Zane mentioning he pierced his wrist on a trip with Carina. Comparing the relationship between Carina and Zane to Vina and myself left me feeling an eerie parallel journey connecting me to Zane.

Vina continued, "You need to understand that the opportunity to help others develop a heightened life experience through clairvoyance, telepathy, and overall celestial magic felt liberating. Watching the wonderment wash over people's faces as they comprehended their newfound abilities left us feeling victorious."

Conway responded, "Unfortunately, others didn't always see it that way, as they were losing faith in our ability to find a cure for their negative reactions. Expectedly, a few betrayed us, breaking the rules of our contracts; some escaped the fortress, sending us on a mission to track them down. Conspiring to break free from our world, they wanted to take our newfound prophecies and evidence to the mundane world in hopes of gaining recognition for their unimaginable gifts or compensation for their negative side effects of the serum.

"Leaving our fortress targeted, rumors from those who escaped triggered investigations from authorities, each time more thorough and each time more difficult to disclose. Knowing our serum could potentially provide disease prevention, clairvoyance, telepathy, rejuvenation and much more, we had hoped to present this to the world with praise. However, with no evidence to cure the side effects, we knew it would only demonize us.

"Embarking on the greatest key to humanity, we had to be extremely careful."

Conway sat up straight. He muttered quietly, "Do you want to question the integrity of the information presented to you?" Hesitantly responding no, unable to articulate my thoughts, I threw myself back into the comfort of the chair cushion. Standing quickly in reaction to my defeat, he returned to his parlor.

The ice cracking as he poured another drink, he said, "Your father and I were best friends." The most profound string of words he had said all night, I took a long deep breath, letting it out slowly as if to release all fear.

CHAPTER
14
THE NINE OF WANDS

Resting my eyes, another vision of the Knight of Cups appeared to me, leading me to believe Carina was trying to reach me. Realizing the image of the Knight of Cups served as a message to trust in Zane. I was left in a state of sanctity.

I forced my eyes open at the sound of Vina's voice, "Maggie, Maggie are you okay?" Sitting up to focus on Vina, I realized I must have passed out. Helping me through the doorway back to the couch, Conway placed a glass of water in front of me. Sipping slowly, I was eager to hear more. Vina repeatedly checked my stability, suggesting I rest before they continued. Unruffled, I insisted they carry on.

Vina and Conway looked at each other in approval, sitting comfortably on the couch across from me.

Vina said, "I need you to recall the night you saw your father being placed in the car."

The imagery was fresh in my mind as if it was yesterday, she explained, "Your father didn't want to leave you, but he had no choice, based on the state of the fortress. We needed his expertise to guide us to a resolution. He had an idea that could revert the negative impacts on the recipients and set us back on track to the original plan. The men who forced your father into the car were hired as a security team. Only appearing harsh to ward off anyone watching from a distance. Your father was very conflicted about leaving his family, and for a brief moment, he seemed to want to run back into the comfort of his home. That is probably the moment you saw the man firmly place his hand on your father's head when forcing him into the car."

Tears filled my eyes as I thought to myself, what has my father done? What kind of place is this? Why would anyone want to tamper with humanity? Of course, all good can come with bad in anyone and everything. Certainly, this plan is faulty.

Vina looked directly at me, throwing her comforting smile toward me. Asking me to listen to the rest, I nodded in confirmation, unable to escape her charming sense of perception. "You must know your parents were fighting because your father was leaving. In hopes of protecting you and your mother from this world until the serum was perfected, he was desperate for a convincing story. Telling your mother he didn't love her anymore shattered your mother's heart. Knowing this was the only way she would never search for him, your father saved you both."

A love so divine, suddenly broken by just a few words.

CHAPTER
15
THREE OF SWORDS

Sudden suspicion took over me as Conway's lack of candor lingered in the background. Realizing I was somehow part of this unimaginable creation, my purpose here was still not exposed. A sixth sense warned me of danger, uttering impulsively, Where is my father?!

After an intimidating glare, Conway spoke without further acknowledging my dismay. "Eagerly waiting for your father to arrive, we feared chaos would break out in the fortress. Watching subjects battle their darkest impulses left us conceding to the possibility that we created criminals. Frantically studying the original artifacts, I was unable to find a solution. Unable to sleep, I spent all night thinking of every conversation Jones (your father) and I had. Falling across a memory of a lock box, I once saw him slip in a drawer, which sent me rifling through every corner of his office. Finally, discovering the box under a loose floorboard, I could pry it open. I felt exalted to find a page he had hidden and removed from the artifact. Reading carefully, I thought it was the answer I was looking for."

Bravely, I interrupted, I asked why my father would hide such an important piece of information.

Conway responded sternly, "Not important," and continued, "The page described combining the serum with a metal chip. The instruction defined the chip as a tracking device. Monitoring the distance between those who were chipped. Understanding this would give us ultimate control of all subjects, I waited impatiently for your father."

Vina, kneeled before my feet, spoke softly, "What I am about to tell you will be painful, please let me explain." The sounds of her voice shaking send palpitations through my heart.

I envisioned myself standing on the edge of the highest point of a rock quarry. No sound, just the view of rock for miles. Sensing a moment of calm before the storm, I took a long deep breath, holding it as long as I could. Letting the air out slowly, I knew nothing can prepare me for what's to come.

Vina whispers, "Your father never made it here. The car he was in exploded. No one made it out alive."

"I am sorry to be the one to tell you this, your father died."

The earth cracked beneath my feet, simultaneously breaking my heart into a million pieces. As the momentum built, so did my heart break. With every fracture in the stone, slashes rip through my soul. The earth convulsed as my body stood completely still. My spiritual being was dying of sadness, and the ground ruthlessly continued to shake. The final eruption sent a longitudinal break through the rock, dividing the floor in two. Looking down at the fork in the path, inconsolable tears poured from my eyes.

CHAPTER
16
THE STAR

An obvious assassination, left me pleading for answers. Needing to know my purpose here, I demanded Vina explain.

Sympathetic, she began, "Your father and Conway were the first to test the serum on themselves. Preoccupied with the excitement of their increasing abilities, your father failed to notice your mother's growing belly. Working away from home for such long periods left her doubting his loyalty. Unable to keep you a secret any longer, your mother announced her pregnancy. Masking his sudden onset of fear, celebrating was a difficult task. Knowing that tampering with his own DNA could have a profound effect on your growth, your development was his greatest concern.

"Watching you closely as you grew, we knew you had natural gifts. You being one of two children ever born to someone injected with a version of the serum is truly magnificent".

"Questioning who else conceived a child after injecting themselves," Conway shouted across the room, introducing himself as the father.

At that moment, my thoughts intersected. I recalled recent memories of unusual occurrences:

I flashed back to critiquing myself in the mirror as bruises and scrapes miraculously healed, leaving my skin more radiant than ever before.

Reliving the night, my frustration reached a final boiling point, slamming my eyes open, annoyed at the light just as it suddenly shut off.

I was in awe when Carina delivered the precise selection of food matching my traditional weekly meal with friends.

Remembering the evening, Zane commented, "I heard you were ready!"

I reminded myself that Vina said, "The interesting thing is that I did not come to you in that dream. You pulled me into it."

This recollection made me realize my spiritual ascension, giving me a sense of clarity.

At the perfect time, I heard Zane's voice, "Maggie, I am Conway's son. I developed my gifts the same way you did. I recently discovered that Carina has been monitoring me since birth. Something has gone wrong here. I discovered that everyone else will need the serum to heighten their state of being, ours will continue to grow naturally. I don't have all the answers yet. I hear your thoughts, and I feel your presence. I will get to you. However, you have to escape."

Learning that Zane was the other child born to a recipient of the serum confirms another comparable experience I shared with Zane.

Taking hold of my composure, I watched Vina and Conway intensely stare at each other from across the room. Conway abruptly broke eye contact and stormed toward the door. He exited the room, slamming the door loudly behind him. Unshaken, Vina marched toward me. Warning me to fight any thought or impulse to escape, she demanded I listen to the rest of the details. With a new sense of my mystic power, holding on to a shred of hope in saving myself, I agreed to hear her out.

CHAPTER
17
EIGHT OF SWORDS

Waiting to hear more about the tracking chip, Vina began. "When your father passed, I knew it was up to Conway and me to find a solution. Knowing whoever assassinated your father would soon be coming for us, I needed to act fast. The blueprint alluded to a location concealing this tracking chip, sending me on a trip to Egypt. It was a long journey presenting many terrible situations that were never to be discussed. With the utmost gratitude to the universe, I found my way to the chip."

Vina, agitated by memories of her journey, I sat quietly waiting for her to continue.

"Upon my return, Conway and I followed the blueprint. Identifying how to recreate the serum and adding DNA from subjects has proven to overcome psychological trauma. The artifacts stipulated that testing the serum with the chip should be done only on a subject born to humans injected with the original serum. The instructions promised a magical response, leading to another change in DNA and, ultimately, a cure.

"We had to bring you here to help us. Please allow us to use your DNA, providing a cure for those in the fortress experiencing psychological distress. You will become the most powerful of all."

Unsteadied by the incomprehensible request, I timidly asked if I have already been injected with this serum.

Vina looked at the floor. I was distracted by Zane's muffled voice pleading, "You have to get out of there. They are lying to you. My mother was in the car with your father! My father is responsible for their deaths!"

My anger built as I thought about how Zane and I were robbed of a parent and these people were responsible.

My demeanor was no longer patient; I looked to Vina demanding answers, interrogating her as I forcefully walked toward her. I could feel my vibration growing with rage as Vina mirrored my actions. My voice raised in my demand for answers, I moved around the room in sudden rage. Vina grabbed hold of me to control my outburst. Pulling at the door, I felt my strength increasing with each tug.

Envisioning ripping the door off its hinges, Vina became unhinged in her lack of control as she yelled, "Stop. The man chasing you on the path was Zane. He is evil. Zane was the one who drugged you and took you to that cement room. He was leaving you there for dead! He is scared that you will become the most powerful of us all, taking his place as leader of this fortress."

Her words gained momentum in my mind, like a volcano erupting inside me. The room blurred around me as the walls started pulling from the floor. Furniture lifted and swirled around the room like a tornado of rage in my heart. The floor beneath me shook like an earthquake as the chaos sent Vina flying into a wall. The impact knocked Vina to the floor, leaving her unconscious.

My rage subsided, and so did the commotion in the room.

The appearance of the upheaval in the room sent my mind to a childhood flashback, living in my family home. I only remembered the look on my mother's face as she entered my playroom to see toys and plastic furniture thrown from one end of the room to the other. Asking me immediately why I had created such a mess, I remembered blaming a friend. No friend was in sight, as my mother stood there with a look of disbelief. Reliving the memory, I believed my mother when she told me I was lying. Unable to convince her I was not responsible, I took the blame, knowing I had no proof of my story. Recalling Vina admitted to her presence in my life since birth, I was suspicious she contributed to the dismay of my playroom that day.

The sounds of people outside the room sent me scanning for a hiding place. I knew someone was going to burst through that door at any moment. Hiding in a small space between two walls, I waited.

Suddenly, a bang, causing an explosion, sent the door flying off its hinges into the wall across the room. Kneeling to the floor to see around the wall, I moved quietly to avoid being heard. Just as I gained sight of the doorway, Zane appeared.

Rushing toward me, he stood firmly in front of me between the walls. Gripping my arms, he intently looked in my eyes as he said, "Vina lied to you, they want to use us to further develop themselves.

"I found a copy of a missing page from the artifact. Your father left it for me to find along with a note. He explained that he only understood the complete artifact after injecting himself with the serum. His newfound intelligence gained from the serum was needed to decipher the big picture. After realizing that anyone born to a recipient of the serum could experience the fate we are experiencing now, he knew he had to hide it. With no one planning children, he believed the serum would provide him with enough intelligence to figure out how to change the outcome. After we were born, your father confided this truth to my mother. Together, they vowed to protect us, concealing the missing page forever. "Maggie, I know of your mysterious symptoms in your mind: sudden jolts, ringing and pressure building in your head. I am experiencing this, too. According to the artifact, it's an effect of the metamorphosis that takes place when we are in close vicinity of each other.

"I was the one in the forest with you, I brought you to the fortress upon my father's instruction. He told me you were a threat to our fortress.

"My loyalty to my father dissolved after finding the missing page from the artifact. I telepathically heard my father tell you about finding the missing page hidden in your father's office. I listened to what he did not say out loud. "He is willing to sacrifice us to save his fortress. He had your father, and my mother killed for trying to protect us.

"Our extraordinary connection and my rapidly developing gifts in your presence were all the proof I needed.

"We are the only two humans born naturally to the effects of the serum. I don't think my father understood how quickly we would develop simultaneously in each other's presence. These last few weeks, they have been monitoring us both very closely, watching our abilities grow and unfold before their eyes.

"We are almost out of time. We have to go now."

CHAPTER
18
THE LOVERS

Cradling me in his arms, he carried me down the winding stairs. Moving as fast as he could, we headed for an exit. As we reached the bottom of the staircase, Zane placed me on my feet. His eyes locked on mine, he said, "Move quickly, they are coming. Stay close. Do not leave my side unless I tell you to."

As we ran to the entrance of the fortress, it was as though the doors were being hammered down from the outside. Zane stopped me and said "They are here."

Pulling me in the opposite direction, he looked for another way out. Yelling for me to move faster, we ran through a long dark corridor that looked like an empty hospital hallway at night. Sounds of the entrance doors bashing to the ground, followed by a multitude of heavy footsteps, sent us fleeing faster.

Jerking me to the ground, Zane moved his fingers along the floor like he was looking for an opening. Pulling a piece of tile from the surface, he tugged on a large metal loop, lifting the board up and revealed a crawl space under the surface.

Guiding me backwards down the hole, my feet reached for grip, finally landing on step. Completely immersed in the floor, Zane stands over me. Placing his hands firmly on each side of my face, I could hear his thoughts loud and clear.

He told me, "They are close. Don't listen to them. Just listen to me. You can block them out, if you focus only on my voice."

"Conway had your father, and my mother killed so he could become the sole ruler of the fortress. He is planning the same fate for us once they complete their research! Together our cells become synergistic.

"The longer we stay in each other's presence, the faster metamorphosis takes over. Together, we will become the most powerful supernatural beings in the world. Scientists working for the fortress surgically placed metal tracking chips in our wrists. To protect themselves from the powerful beings we will become, they must track the distance between us to prevent us from being together. The night on the terrace, I wasn't sure what I felt in my wrist. I couldn't tell you with my father watching and listening in the distance. Grasping your wrist later, I was sure you were experiencing the same sensation.

"We have to stay away from each other if we are going to live any kind of normal life. If they find us, we will be test subjects for the rest of our lives. Our powers grow in each other's presence, so who knows what supernatural creatures we will become?

"I hear you always. I feel your presence. If you need me, I will get to you.

"We must stay away from each other until I can find a way for us to be together.

"Trust no one. I will see you again. You must go now!"

Despite his words, I only wanted to be with him. With no clear path out in sight, I begged him to stay with me. Just as I finished speaking, I could hear thumping feet getting closer.

Zane pressed his lips against mine. Just like that, the whole world stopped. The love I felt for him was mirrored right back at me. Divinely connected, I knew I would see him again. Slowly pulling away, he directed me to move down the steps. As Zane placed the board back on the floor, our eyes were locked until his face disappeared through the smallest crack.

For the first time, our minds were silent.

CHAPTER
19
SEVEN OF SWORDS

The ground was uneven, wet and cold. I rolled to my side, leaves and branches peeled from my bare legs. I pried my heavy eyes open, struggling to focus on my surroundings. I jumped to my feet, I have been here before! At the edge of the forest, I could see a familiar road. Running toward it as fast as I could, I knew how to get home.

With my driveway in view, I ran faster. Bursting through the door, I called out to my mother. She peeked around the corner, saying, "I'm right here. What's wrong?" I was shocked by her calmness, I asked myself why she was unconcerned. I have been gone for weeks. Questioning her lack of worry, she responded, "Worried? You have only been gone two hours? Lyra and Van have been calling to ask if you are going to the pub with them tonight."

So confused. Was it all a dream?

Nothing made sense. I was too afraid to tell my mother everything that happened. She tried to calm me down. Running the bath for me, she assured me it would help. Placing a towel on the counter, she left me alone to collect my thoughts. Looking down at my muddy white tank top and jean shorts, I thought of the forest. I slowly entered the warm bath and threw the clothes in a nearby hamper. The surrounding warmth was comforting as I lay my head back, resting on the basin.

I asked myself over and over how these memories could be a dream. It seemed so real. I slowly move my body further to the end of the tub as I plunged my head under water to drown out the noise.

Feeling a sense of safety in my mother's home, I was relieved at the thought of it all being a dream. Thoughts of not knowing what happened to me during those two hours, left me with lingering anxiety.

Remembering my mother was in the next room brought me some relief as I knew I could tell her everything.

Still holding my breath underwater, I was startled by the sound of Conway's voice in my head, "Maggie, you can never escape. No matter where you go, we will always find you.

"Every thought that passes through your mind, we will hear."

"Nothing you think or do will ever be private."

Forcing my head out of the water and taking a deep breath, "I know this terror is real."

Conway's voice echoes, "Maggie, you can't control anything.

"You have been chipped and injected with the serum. You will live in your world for now."

The horror took hold of me as I scratched the surface of my skin. Puncturing the skin on my wrist, blood poured into the tub. Frantically digging through my skin for the chip with my nails, I found myself dizzy from the sight of the blood.

"We will find you wherever you are and eventually bring you back to the fortress.

"You are going to save our society. Just remember, we can hear everything you think and say.

"Telling anyone will only harm them."

I let out a loud scream, and pulled my hands to my ears in an effort to keep the voices out. Physically present at home, I was completely alone in my thoughts.
Psychologically present in the fortress, my mind was forever exposed.

- Properstrious surveillance.

CHAPTER
20
THE WHEEL OF FORTUNE

I opened my eyes to a room filled with bright lights. Focusing my vision, I realized I am lying in a hospital bed. I was wearing cream-colored pants and shirt, no socks on my feet and a bandage on my wrist. My mother walked toward my bed, and sat calmly beside me. Where am I? Nervously tucking my sheets in around me, she is startled by a knock at the door, sending her abruptly to the room's entrance. Trying to see who was there, I moved back and forth to get a view around her. She made one small move to the right, revealing Conway in the doorway. The shock on my face sent him straight toward me, introducing himself as Conway Clarke. Bewildered by the introduction, I was speechless. Standing over me, he asked, "Maggie, do you know why you are here?" To protect my mother's innocence in this, I respond no. Remembering his threats to tell no one, I am unsure of what else to say.

Speaking to me as if this was our first encounter, he explained that my father's death took such a toll on my mental health, and my mother had no choice but to admit me to the hospital for severe depression leading to psychosis. Sitting upright, I lost control of my composure. Yelling at him, I blamed him for my father's death. I accused him of having my father assassinated to protect and gain control of his fortress. Conway, appearing concerned, yelled for the nurse to assist. To my dismay, Carina barrels through the door to my bedside. Proceeding to hold me down, I am distraught at the sight of the hotel maid. She frantically told me she was the nurse only trying to help me. "Please calm down, Maggie. I am here to help you. You have been asleep for many hours. You need your strength. Can I please bring you something to eat?"

Out of control, I flailed around the bed in an effort to get away from her. Holding me down, she injected me with something. Immediately I became sleepy, the drug forced my body to relax back into the bed.

Looking at my mother, I could see tears fill her eyes as she reached for my hand. She explained that the authorities found me unconscious in the forest after I received the news of my father's death. She proceeded to tell me that my father was in a terrible accident on his way home from work. The crash led to a gas leak, which caused an explosion he was unable to escape from. Arguing, I told her he was assassinated by someone Conway hired. She calmly interrupted, telling me I had told her that story many times before. Confused, I asked her why I had no memory of this. She told me my memory loss was expected based on the treatments I had received.

Treatment? What kind of treatment?

With a delayed response, she said electroshock therapy. "The shock and grief you experienced were not treatable any other way. You were allergic to all forms of medication available to treat your depression and psychosis. Electroshock was our only option."

Scanning every memory, I waited for the sudden jolt and ringing in my ears to deflect me from this moment. Waiting, I realized this sensation was not present. I was horrified by the thought that the jolts, ringing and pressure derived from the electroshock therapy and not the momentum of my synergistic build-up of my supernatural connection with Zane.

Sick to my stomach, I heard Conway mention that he will bring my psychologist. Unsurprised a psychologist is on the way, I looked toward the door to see Vina standing there. Disillusioned, Vina introduced herself to me as my psychologist.

Everything seemed clinical, I still could not stop thinking of Zane. A love that carried through to this moment could not be made up. I wondered if he would enter the room as a whole other person. Asking those around me, Where is Zane? Genuine confusion took over their expressions. My mother said, "We have never heard of Zane."

I held back further communication, fearing I would be sent for another round of electroshock. Turning away from everyone, I rolled on my side, and stared at the doorway. Conway directed everyone out of the room, advising them I needed time to adjust. Alone, I lay still comparing the thoughts of each reality. With the hallway in my view, a shadow filled the doorway.

With the darkness broken by Zane's face, I sat up quickly in hopes he was real.

He threw a quick wink at my soul and disappeared.

Searching the hallway to find no one, sent me back to my bed sadly. With my head in my hands, I thought of possibilities to make sense of all this. My hopeful mind swirled around parallel universes, wormholes and destiny while tugging at the dreadful conclusion of this hospital.
I must be losing my mind.
I lay my head on the pillow, tortured by my thoughts.
I hoped I would just fall asleep. I needed relief from this reality.
With only the sounds of hospital equipment beeping in the distance, loneliness consumed me.
Breaking the despair, the sound of Zane's voice whispered, "Maggie, trust the process."

EPILOGUE

Maggie convoluted in her purpose within the universe and those who are part of her journey, she holds on firmly to her trust in the process.